First published by V&A Publishing, 2015
Victoria and Albert Museum
South Kensington
London SW7 2RL
www.vandapublishing.com

Ilaria Demonti's illustrations published
courtesy of Debbie Bibo Agency.

Hardback edition
ISBN 978 1 85177 830 0

10 9 8 7 6 5 4 3 2 1
2019 2018 2017 2016 2015

A catalogue record for this book is available
from the British Library.

Every effort has been made to seek permission to
reproduce those images whose copyright does not reside
with the V&A, and we are grateful to the individuals
and institutions who have assisted in this task. Any
omissions are entirely unintentional, and the details
should be addressed to V&A Publishing.

Printed in China

V&A Publishing
Supporting the world's leading
museum of art and design,
the Victoria and Albert
Museum, London

WENDY AND THE WALLPAPER CAT

WRITTEN BY JASON HOOK
ILLUSTRATIONS BY ILARIA DEMONTI

V&A PUBLISHING

Mum said it was bedtime.
Dad said it was bedtime.
Wendy said she wasn't tired.
Then Mum said it really *was* bedtime.

Wendy snuggled up. She closed
her eyes tightly. And she waited …
and waited.

But the more Wendy tried to sleep,
the less sleepy she felt.

It was just like the night before.
And the night before that.

Wendy tried everything …

counting sheep …

turning cartwheels …

dancing on her bed …

reading her nursery rhymes ...

turning the lights off ...

turning the lights on ...

... but nothing worked.

When the sun came up, Wendy had not slept a wink.

She said, 'Good Morning, Mum!' and, 'Good Morning, Dad!'
with her best smile. But Mum shook her head, and Dad
scratched his chin.

'We're taking you to stay with
Grandpa Walter,' said Mum.

Wendy loved her Grandpa Walter.

She loved the bedtime stories he told
when he came to visit her. But she
had never been to his house before.

And what a strange house it was.
It had the prettiest garden Wendy
had ever seen. But everything was so
neat and so tidy that it looked more
like a painting than a garden.

When Grandpa Walter opened the door, he was wearing a green suit that looked just like his garden. 'Welcome to my world of wonderful wallpapers!' said Walter. 'I wonder which room will be your favourite.'

All the walls
in Walter's house
were covered with
beautiful paper.

Walking upstairs,
Wendy looked up at
the roses on the walls.
When she reached up to
touch them, a red petal
fluttered down.

'I can smell the roses!'
said Wendy.

'Well! Well!' said Walter,
'How wonderful!'

Wendy walked into the first bedroom and looked up at the starfish and seashells on the walls.

When she reached up to touch the wallpaper, a trickle of sand poured down.

'I can smell the sea!' said Wendy.

'Well! Well!' said Walter, 'How wild!'

And Wendy wondered if this
might be her favourite room.

Wendy walked into the second bedroom and looked up at the leaves on the walls. When she reached up to touch the wallpaper, an orange fell down into her hand.

'I can taste oranges!' said Wendy.

'Well! Well!' said Walter, 'How mouth-watering!'

And Wendy wondered if this might be her favourite room.

Wendy walked into the third bedroom, which was covered in cobwebs. She looked up at the wallpaper, and saw all the characters from her favourite nursery rhymes.

Wendy knew at once that this was her favourite room.

'I wish I could sleep in here!' she said.

'Well, you can!' said Walter, 'What a wonderful choice!'

That evening, Wendy couldn't wait
for bedtime.

She read her book of nursery rhymes,
and looked up at the wallpaper.

She saw a blue cat playing a fiddle,
a cow jumping over the moon,
a little dog laughing and a dish
running away with a spoon.

With so many wonderful things to look at,
Wendy didn't know how she would ever get to sleep …

Wendy reached up to touch the wallpaper. She heard the sound of a fiddle and saw the blue cat leap down from the wall.

He looked so much fun, she couldn't help running after him.

She chased the blue cat through
a forest of orange trees.

Wendy chased the blue cat across a golden
beach covered with starfish and seashells.

She chased him around and
around a bed of red roses.

Wendy chased the blue cat around
and around Grandpa Walter's garden.

And when at last she caught up
with the cat, he played his
fiddle and they danced together
the whole night long.

'Good morning!' said
Grandpa Walter,
'Did you sleep well?'

'Oh, I didn't sleep at all,'
said Wendy. 'I danced
the whole night long!'

'Well! Well!' said Walter,
'How wonderful!'

When Mum came to
pick her up, Wendy
said, 'My favourite
room had a blue cat
playing a fiddle and
a cow jumping over
the Moon!'

'Well! Well!' said Mum. 'That was
my room when I was little!'

Back home, Dad had decorated Wendy's room with beautiful new wallpaper. Now, Wendy couldn't wait for bedtime.

When she reached up to touch the wall, Wendy wondered about the wallpaper cat. Then, she heard the sound of a fiddle being played.

'Well! Well!' said Wendy. 'How wonderful!'

That night, dreaming of
Walter's wonderful wallpaper,
Wendy slept wonderfully well.

And so did Mum and Dad.

WENDY AND WALTER

The patterns shown in Grandpa Walter's house are from real wallpapers. They were all designed by the English artist Walter Crane (1845–1915) and many of his wallpapers can be seen by appointment in the Prints & Drawings Study Room at the Victoria and Albert Museum. Crane was one of the best-known illustrators of books for children in Victorian times, when his work gained popularity through mass-produced picture books known as 'toy books'. He was also an examiner at the South Kensington Museum, which is now the Victoria and Albert Museum.

In the 1870s, it became popular to decorate nurseries with wallpapers that were intended to stir children's imaginations. Many designs featured pictures from fairytales and nursery rhymes, and Crane's wallpapers included 'Sleeping Beauty' (1879) and 'The House That Jack Built' (1886). His designs for young and old were fashionable both at home and abroad, and American author Mark Twain was among those who used a Walter Crane design, 'Miss Mouse At Home' (1877), to decorate his children's nursery.

An article written in 1884 said of Walter Crane's wallpapers: 'With the aid of a little intelligent and sympathetic talk, nursery walls, covered with these designs, might be made to live within the lives of children.'

The Walter Crane wallpapers that come to life in *Wendy and the Wallpaper Cat* are:

1. 'The Formal Garden' wallpaper. This shows a tree in a planter on a plinth, surrounded by foliage, poppies and white lilies. It is a colour woodblock print on paper, made in 1904 by Jeffrey & Co. (E.5101-1919)

2. 'Saxon' wallpaper. This has a repeat pattern of red roses on a cream background. It is a colour woodblock print on paper, made in 1909 by Jeffrey & Co. (E.2324-1932)

3. 'Seashore' wallpaper dado. This has a pattern of shells and starfish on sand. It is a colour woodblock print on paper, made in 1879 by Jeffrey & Co. (E.4029-1915)

4. 'Orange Tree' wallpaper. This shows the fruit and foliage of an orange tree. It is a colour woodblock print on paper, made in 1902 by Jeffrey & Co. (E.5140-1919)

5. 'Nursery Rhymes' wallpaper. This shows characters from nursery rhymes including Humpty Dumpty, Little Miss Muffet, Little Jack Horner and the cat with his fiddle from Hey Diddle Diddle. It is a colour machine print on paper, made in 1876 by Jeffrey & Co. (E.42A-1971)

1.   2.   3.   4.   5.

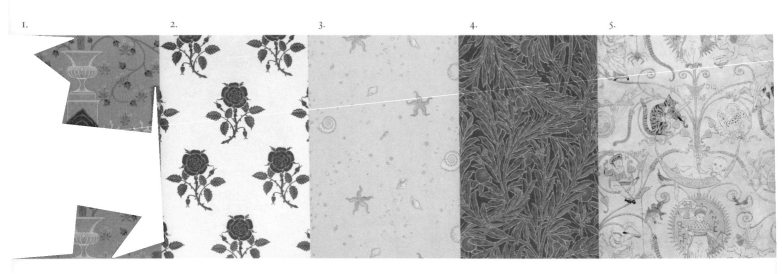